8/96

SWEET, SWEET
FIG BANANA

SWEET, SWEET
FIG BANANA

Phillis Gershator

Illustrations by

Fritz Millevoix

Albert Whitman & Company, Morton Grove, Illinois

Dedicated to the aspiring readers at
Dober Elementary School, St. Thomas, Virgin Islands,
and my editors, Judith Mathews and Kathy Tucker —P.G.

For Moise Millevoix —F.M.

Library of Congress Cataloging-in-Publication Data

Gershator, Phillis.
Sweet, sweet fig banana / written by Phillis Gershator ;
illustrated by Fritz Millevoix.
p.   cm.
Summary: Soto takes some of the bananas he has grown to share
with his friends at the Market Square where his mother works.
ISBN 0-8075-7693-X
[1. Banana—Fiction. 2. Caribbean Area—Fiction.]
I. Millevoix, Fritz, ill. II. Title.
PZ7.G316Sw   1996   95-32087
  [E]—dc20   CIP
                                                  AC

Designed by Lucy Smith.
The text of this book is set in Caxton Light.
The illustrations are rendered in acrylic paint.

Phillis Gershator was born in New York, grew up in California, and now lives on St. Thomas, in the Virgin Islands. In all these places she has loved books. She is a librarian and writer, and has written several picture books.

Fig bananas are what small, fat, yellow bananas are called in the Virgin Islands. Phillis has grown them right near her house.

Fritz Millevoix was born in Port-au-Prince, Haiti. He moved to the United States in 1990 and now lives in Chicago.

Fritz began painting when he was fourteen. He studied art in Haiti, and prefers to paint in a primitive, or very simple, style, using bright, happy colors.

Fritz Millevoix's work has been shown in the United States, Haiti, Italy, and Germany. This is his first book for children.

Soto planted a baby banana shoot in the yard.

One morning, after a big rain, he saw a leaf poking up from the shoot like a roll of green paper. The next day the leaf unfurled, then another leaf and another.

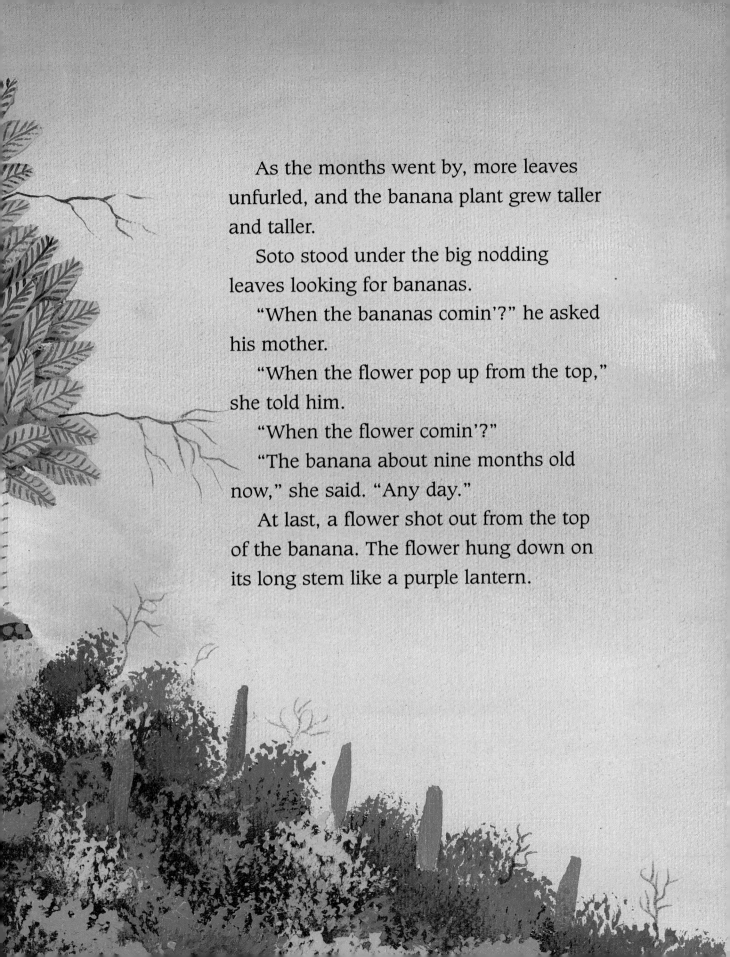

As the months went by, more leaves unfurled, and the banana plant grew taller and taller.

Soto stood under the big nodding leaves looking for bananas.

"When the bananas comin'?" he asked his mother.

"When the flower pop up from the top," she told him.

"When the flower comin'?"

"The banana about nine months old now," she said. "Any day."

At last, a flower shot out from the top of the banana. The flower hung down on its long stem like a purple lantern.

Soto watched the tiny green bananas growing from the flower stem, and he kept his eye out for the tree rat and the thrushee. The tree rat and greedy thrushee were watching the bananas, just like Soto, waiting for them to turn yellow.

"When the bananas gettin' yellow?" Soto asked his mother.

"You stop watchin' every day, and they surprise you."

When the little green bananas got fat, Soto told his mother, "Let we cut the bananas."

"I know you watchin' and waitin' a long, long time, Soto," his mother said. "But they still green."

"Look at the top, Mommy. Some bananas almost yellow. And the tree rat and thrushee hangin' round."

Sure enough, Soto's mother heard a rustling in the bush. So she cut down the heavy bunch of bananas and carried it into the house, safe from the tree rat and the thrushee.

Soto's mother was a market lady. She went to Market Square every day. She sold lottery tickets, fruits and vegetables, and candies from a jar. Soto kept his mother company.

Then he walked around looking at the
other people in Market Square selling fruits
and vegetables, fresh fish, soda, fruit juice,
and T-shirts.

Today, Soto watched the hat man making hats.
The hat man wove the strips of a palm frond together into a big hat. "It hot, man, without a hat," he said, and he put one on Soto's head. "Good thing you come by today, man. You my walkin' advertisement."

Then Soto watched the fraico man shave ice for fraicos. A fraico looked so cool on a hot day! The ice was piled up in a paper cup with fruit syrup on top. The fraico man had all kinds of syrup—lemon, lime, mango, guava . . .

"Soto, you watchin' me like a thrushee," the fraico man said. He gave Soto a lime fraico for free. Soto made it last a long time.

Then Soto ran over to the library, one block from Market Square. He sat at a table looking at picture books. When he went to school, like his brother, he would be able to read the words.

He liked to look at books about airplanes. Lots of airplanes flew around his island: helicopters, sea planes, and jets.

The librarian showed Soto a brand new book about airplanes. She pointed to the word "airplanes" on the cover. When she turned the page, Soto found the word "airplane" all by himself.

By the time Soto got home, two of the bananas had already turned yellow!

"The bananas gettin' ripe, Soto," his mother said. "They fat little fig bananas. Soon they all soft and sweet, the sweetest of sweet, sweet bananas!"

When Soto heard that, he said, "Mommy, when they ripe, I want three hands."

Each small bunch of bananas on the big bunch was a "hand." Soto's bunch had six hands, and each hand had ten fingers!

"Three? You eat *one* hand all at once, you get a bellyache," his mother warned him. "What you want with *three*?"

"It a surprise," Soto said.

When the bananas turned yellow, Soto and his mother took them to Market Square. Everyone who passed by bought some sweet, ripe fig bananas. They were selling so fast, Soto was afraid he wouldn't get any. Now there were only three hands left!

"Mommy, I want three hands," he reminded her.

"They sellin' quick, Soto. We makin' money."

"Please."

"Oh, all right. You the one planted the banana. But what you plan on doin' with three hands?"

Soto just smiled. He carefully picked up the last three hands.

He gave one to the hat man.

"Hmm, fig bananas!" said the hat man. "Sweeter than sugar cane!" The hat man went right to work, weaving a palm frond bowl to put them in.

Soto gave one hand to the fraico man.

"Bananas been around since man began, and sweet, sweet fig bananas the best," the fraico man said. "My favorite fruit!"

Soto gave one hand to the librarian.

"This *is* a surprise!" she said.

She peeled one banana. "What a thin peel!" Then she took a bite. "This is the tastiest banana I ever tasted!"

"It a fig banana," Soto said.

He told the librarian how he planted the banana shoot in his yard. "It come from the bottom of the mother plant. It take a long, long time for the banana tree to grow, like a baby grow. Then the flower pop out the top. Then the little bananas grow. You know who want a bite? The tree rat and the thrushee! That why we cut the stem and take the bananas in the house. Then they turn yellow, fast, fast, fast."

"Soto, it's like a story in a book!" the librarian said. She wrote it all down. She gave the story a title: "Soto's Fig Banana."

Soto copied the letters neatly: S-O-T-O'S F-I-G B-A-N-A-N-A. He drew the pictures, too.

"I knew you were going to read and write pretty soon, Soto. But I did not know you were already an artist! Could I have a picture for the library?"

"Yes," Soto said.

And every time Soto went to look at books, there was his picture hanging on the wall: a beautiful fig banana!